Black Bart is Dead

A Captain Finn Treasure Mystery

Book 2

LIZ DODWELL

Liz Dodwell

Black Bart is Dead: A Captain Finn Treasure Mystery
Copyright © 2014 by Liz Dodwell
www.lizdodwell.com

Print ISBN-13: 978-1-939860-14-9
Published by Mix Books, LLC

Table of Contents

Liz Dodwell

For Fizz
A living treasure

Cast of Characters

A Who's Who of the Characters and their pirate party aliases.

Captain Rex Finsmer: Usually called Finn or Captain Finn. A famous and well-respected shipwreck treasure hunter, also known for his ability as an amateur sleuth. He's attending as his alter ego, **'Everyone's favorite pirate.'**

Phillida Jane Trent (Phill): Finn's thirty-something sidekick. She's actually more of a protegee to him and lives with him on Time Voyager. Her party character is **Anne Dieu-le-Veut**, a 17th century French pirate.

Elbert Lex Van Nifterik (Bert): An internet and gaming genius who has made millions even though he's only in his early twenties. His home is on Mud Bug Island, where the party is being held. His choice of pirate is **Barbarossa**.

Monks: Bert's butler and jack of all trades. His chosen character is the infamous **Blackbeard**.

Delia Beaton Baynes (Dilly): The event organizer; attractive, but not known for her intellect. She is costumed as the pirate, **Lady Mary Killigrew**.

Ken Kinimaka: A retired college professor of Hawaiian and Japanese descent. He is **Black Bart**.

Dodo Kinimaka: Wife of Ken. She is a children's author and illustrator. Fairly shy and quiet she has made the surprising choice to attend as **Ching Shih**, a female prostitute who became one of the most powerful pirates in history.

Ralph Westgate: A wealthy and rather pompous man in his fifties. His character is **Calico Jack**.

Leticia Westgate: Ralph's long-suffering wife, though she can be determined when called for. Her pirate choice is **Anne Bonny**.

Wayne Gregory: An ex-military man, about the same age as the Kinimakas. He has made the unusual choice to attend as **Suds Merrick**, a New York river pirate.

Eli Shain: A young man who calls himself an independent reporter, he can be quite abrasive. For his pirate character he has dressed as **Moses Cohen Enriques Eanes**.

Teresa: A young woman hired for the evening to help serve the dinner. She is dressed as a simple **pirate wench**.

Liz Dodwell

ONE

Calico Jack had sipped a little too much grog. The overly bright eyes, flushed cheeks and raised voice were enough of a giveaway without Anne Bonny, one hand on hip, the other on the hilt of her sword, telling him in a hissed whisper to 'Sober up!'

Frankly, I found it rather amusing. After all, we were pirates – at least for the night – weren't we supposed to be a bunch of rum-swigging, dissolute ruffians?

Perhaps I'd better explain. Finn and I were guests at a pirate murder mystery dinner on Mud Bug Island, the private hideaway of Elbert Lex Van Nifterik, who goes by Bert. There were 10 of us, plus the butler and maid, all decked out in appropriate pirate garb and punctuating our speech with lots of 'aye ayes' and 'aarghs.'

It all began with SAV. That's an acronym for *Service Animals for Vets* - pronounced SAVE - a charitable organization that rescues animals from shelters and trains them as guide dogs, mobility assistance dogs and hearing assistance dogs for disabled military veterans. It's a great concept; people rescue animals and in return the animals rescue people.

Finn had been the guest speaker at a recent fundraising event for SAV. The other star of the show was a beautiful black labrador, Luna, who had been rescued from a high-kill shelter the day before she was scheduled to be put down. Now she was in training with a local foster family. Anyway, that was when we met Bert.

At just 12 years of age, Bert was designing – and selling - video games, most of them with a pirate theme. At 17 he speculated by buying bitcoin, a virtual currency, when it was less than a dollar and for the next few years watched it rise in value to over $1,000. Not surprisingly, now in his early twenties, Bert is worth millions.

The organizer of the event was Delia Beaton Baynes, otherwise known as Dilly. The minute she opened her mouth I started thinking of her as Silly Dilly. She was a good-looking woman, well put together, with the intellect of a jellyfish and the tentacles to match. She was all over Finn, clinging to him tighter than a limpet to a rock. Not that it's unusual for women to be drawn to Finn. He's a guy you might say is ruggedly handsome, but his real attraction is that he genuinely likes women. He listens to them and he appreciates them. In Dilly's case, though, she was after someone she thought had money and status.

Finn is a shipwreck treasure hunter. That's what his talks are about. His full name is Rex Finsmer but nobody ever calls him Rex; it's always Finn or Captain Finn. I'm Phillida Jane Trent – you can call me Phill – and I work with Finn. I also live on his boat, *Time Voyager,* with him. Although we're not related, he's like a father to me. In fact, he's the only family I have.

At the SAV event we'd set up a display of treasures, many of which were for sale, the proceeds going to the charity. Bert had purchased several high ticket items, and spent some time chatting with Finn. Seems he was quite enamored of pirates and treasure hunting and had come to the event specifically to meet Finn. When Dilly realized Bert was the wealthy recluse of Mud Bug Island fame, she immediately pounced on him, insisting he host another event. He did his best to decline, but was no match for Dilly. And when she came up with the idea of a pirate mystery dinner, he agreed to it only on condition that Finn was in attendance.

So here we were. Finn as himself, in the pirate costume he wore for his visits to the Children's Hospital, where he was known as 'the kids' favorite pirate.' I'd decided to go as Anne Dieu-le-Veut. In 1683, her buccaneer husband was killed by another pirate, Laurens de Graff, in a bar fight. To avenge her husband's death Anne challenged Laurens to a duel. Laurens refused to fight a woman but promptly proposed to her instead. From then on they lived as husband and wife and commanded their pirate ship together. When Laurens was later killed, Anne took his place as Captain. She seemed like a woman I would have liked. *Just saying.*

We were gathered in the great room of Bert's island home, waiting for the game to begin. Originally, Bert had planned to hold the event on his yacht, but weather got in the way of that. Tropical storm Darla was being spiteful, and threatening to claw her way around the Keys, so Bert came in his launch to pick us up from the mainland. The mood had been light-hearted as we waited at the public dock, decked out in our pirate duds. Tourists gawped at us and we gave them a show of pistol-toting, saber-waving bluster until Bert, as Barbarossa, the fierce 16th century Barbary pirate, pulled alongside yelling 'Avast, me hearties!'

One young woman had kept herself apart from the rest of us. An elfin little thing, looking awkward and shy in her wench's costume. I'd introduced myself and she told me her name was Teresa and that she had been hired to assist for the evening as a maid. I tried to draw her into conversation but her every response to my comments was monosyllabic, so I decided to leave her to herself.

Mud Bug is less than six miles offshore and a 20 minute boat ride. There's a natural horseshoe-shaped basin on the east side with extensive dockage. Monks, who is Bert's English butler-cum-factotum was there to greet us and help tie up. He was the only other person on the island, and once we were ashore, he led us into the main house. It wasn't what I expected; especially for a young guy. The walls were white, presumably in deference to the warm climate, and the style of the home modern, but the woodwork and wood flooring were in variegated tones of sunflower blond to rich cocoa and had an aged quality to them. Patterned rugs in Dresden blue and white were scattered around and the furniture was an eclectic mix of Chippendale, Victorian and Louis XVI. Not that I'm any expert, mind you, but I've watched my share of *Antiques Road Show* episodes.

"The flooring and the doors are reclaimed chestnut wood from a monastery in Tuscany."

I hadn't noticed Bert come up behind me. "You brought wood all the way from Italy?"

"Why not? It's beautiful. I thought it deserved to be showcased, rather than chopped up for firewood."

Couldn't argue with that.

"Would you care for a Mud Bug Special, madam?" I heard Monks speak and looked around to see who he was addressing before I realized it was me. *Madam?* That made me feel almost as old as the monastery doors.

I eyed the drinks tray he held out. "There are wormy-looking things that seem to be trying to escape from the glasses."

"Yes, madam. Gummy worms soaked in dark rum. A little black food coloring is added to the rum so the worms take on a more natural 'buggy' appearance."

OK, now I was officially interested. "And what's in the muddy concoction?"

"Spiced rum, Amarula cream, Kahlua, Canton ginger liqueur and fresh lime juice."

"Sounds a bit on the sweet side for a pre-dinner beverage."

"I think, madam, you will find the tartness of the lime and the quantity of spiced rum will balance out the sweetness."

And indeed I did. The drink was delicious, and boozy gummy worms might be one of my new favorite things.

"Why Blackbeard?"

"Madam?"

"You are Blackbeard, aren't you?" I eyeballed the coils of black facial hair and the daggers and pistols stuffed into sashes crisscrossing his chest.

"Quite so. It seemed appropriate to play the part of another Englishman, and Edward Teach – that's Blackbeard's real name – and I have something more in common: we both come from the port town of Bristol. Now, if you will excuse me…" And in a very un-Blackbeard-like manner, Monks gracefully eased himself away, leaving me with Bert.

"I think that dreadful woman," Bert lifted his chin in Dilly's direction, "is after Finn. Should we help him?"

I followed his gaze and watched Dilly leading Finn round like a prize heifer – or should I say bull? – introducing him to the others with an air of 'he's mine, don't touch him.'

"Nah. He can take care of himself." Secretly, I was enjoying his discomfort. "She's just an over-sexed vixen."

"There's more to it than that."

"Why monsieur," I affected my best French piratess accent, "do tell."

"According to my sources.…" I gave Bert one of those 'get real' looks. "Oh, alright. According to Monks – he gets all the local dirt from Wicked Wally's tavern on the mainland – Dilly was married to a man 30 years her senior. When he died he had certain provisos in his will that ensured her, shall we say, constancy."

"So he bribed her."

"Well, yes. I suppose you could call it that. She has a lifetime interest in their home and a reasonable allowance, provided she raises a minimum $100,000 a year for hubby's favorite charity, SAV."

"Wow. That's a bit stiff. But can't she just put some of her allowance towards it? "

"Apparently not. And, of course, if she remarries, she loses everything and has to pay back whatever allowance she's received to date."

"Surely that can't be legal?"

"Her husband was a judge, so he should know."

"The judge was a mean old bastard! I actually feel a little sorry for her. No wonder she's all over Finn. She needs a rich new husband as soon as possible to get her out of this before she's in too deep. Perhaps I should warn him."

Before I had a chance to do so, the sound of a gong crashed through the room, followed by Monks' monotone voice, "Dinner is served."

Liz Dodwell

TWO

The meal was outstanding. Of course, it should be at the $5,000 guests were paying. Bert had picked up the bill for me and Finn; no way did we have $10,000 for dinner, even if it was for a good cause. As organizer, I assumed Dilly did not pay, but Bert had pledged an additional $5,000 per head, so SAV would get close to $100,000 for the night, which meant that Dilly's quota for this year was already safe. The person who solved the mystery stood to win a weekend of treasure diving with Finn, and a shipwreck artifact donated by Bert.

As we chomped our way through pepper-crusted grass-fed filet mignon and a Peruvian version of bouillabaisse with lobster, the group chatted amiably. Dilly had suggested we introduce ourselves when we first sat down, so we'd gone around the table giving our names and pirate pseudonyms.

Dilly began, announcing she was Lady Mary Killigrew. Daughter of a pirate, and married to a former pirate in the 1500s, Lady Mary continued to engage in piracy whenever her husband was away from home. She didn't seem an appropriate character for Dilly, who was the kind of woman to have a panic attack just breaking a nail.

Next to Dilly was Eli Shain, a rather timid-looking young man who chose as his persona Moses Cohen Henriques Eanes, a Sephardic pirate who helped capture

the Spanish treasure fleet in the battle of the Bay of
Matanzas in Cuba in 1628. Who knew there were Jewish
pirates?

Ralph and Leticia Westgate smacked of wealth.
Not in an ostentatious way like Dilly, or a self-made
entrepreneur like Bert, but more like 'old money' people
who'd grown up privileged and simply accepted their
elite status as their birthright. They'd come as Calico Jack
and Anne Bonny. Jack plied his pirating trade in the early
18th century in the Bahamas. In 1720 two women were
part of his crew. One of them was Anne. They became an
item but it didn't last long as Jack was caught and hanged
later the same year. According to one source, Anne's last
words to Jack were, "sorry to see you there, but if you'd
fought like a man, you would not have been hang'd like a
dog." *Ouch*. I hoped Ralph and Leticia had a more loving
relationship.

Another single guy, Wayne Gregory, was at the
table in the guise of Suds Merrick, a New York River
pirate with the Hook Gang. I'd never heard of river
pirates but, apparently, in the late 19th century, the Hook
Gang would hijack shipping along the waterfront. Wayne
carried himself like a military man – I should know, I was
in the army for a few years. He was probably sixtyish, but
kept himself in really good shape. There was no ring on
his wedding finger and he made no mention of a Mrs.
Gregory.

Last was Ken Kinimaka with his wife Dodo. Ken
was retired. He'd been an associate professor in history

and East Asian languages and civilizations. Dodo was a children's book author and illustrator. She was a tiny woman with soft, slender oriental features and a bird-like aura about her, as if she might break if you held her too tightly. She and Ken had chosen Black Bart and Ching Shih as their alter egos. Black Bart was one of the most successful pirates of the 'Golden Age of Piracy' at the beginning of the 1700s. Ching Shih was a major badass; a Chinese prostitute who rose to be a ruthless pirate in the 19th century. I wondered if the seemingly mild-mannered Dodo had a latent savage streak.

Two things of note happened as we sat at the table, and both involved Ken Kinimaka. When he announced he'd taught at Arizona State University, the Westgates had given each other a wide-eyed, startled look. Ralph had begun to say something but Leticia put her hand over his and gave a slight shake of her head. An unspoken resolve seemed to pass between them before they turned their attention back to the table.

A little later, as Monks leaned over to pour wine for Ken, a gold chain fell from inside his open-necked pirate shirt. A bezeled gold coin hung from it.

"That's a gold eagle!" Ken stated. "There's a story in my family that one of my ancestors found a cache of gold eagle coins on the island of Kauai, back in the mid-1800s."

Monks' free hand grabbed for the coin as it swung back and forth and suddenly some of the wine was splashed across the table.

"I'm so terribly sorry, sir. Please pardon my clumsiness. I'll clean this up immediately."

"There's no harm," Ken said. "The only thing that suffered was the table cloth."

"Really, sir, I do apologize."

"Monks," Bert spoke up, "it's fine. Just leave it."

Monks backed away, still apologizing.

"Well that's one for the books." Bert spoke to no-one in particular. "I've never seen Monks get flustered before."

"Who cares about that? I want to know more about Ken's treasure." Dilly looked expectantly at Ken and all eyes followed her lead.

"There's little I know to tell. My family is Hawaiian, if you hadn't already guessed, and the story is about the opium trade in 1846.

"The schooner, Spec, transported opium from Singapore to Hawaii, where it was transferred to another vessel for shipment to San Francisco. The cargo was paid for in gold eagle coins, $100,000 worth, which were loaded on the Spec. The next day, she set sail but got caught in a storm and went down between the islands of Kauai and Niihau."

"Then how did your ancestor find the coins on the island?" Eli Shain couldn't keep the skepticism from his voice.

"Ah," Ken smiled slyly, "two crewmen survived, miraculously overcoming the gale force winds and strong currents that broke apart the Spec in 700 fathoms of water…. so the story goes. But, as it was told to me, those two crewmen were never on board. Somehow, they smuggled the coins to shore before the Spec departed - or perhaps they never loaded them to begin with - and hid them on the island."

"Are you saying Monks' coin is one of the gold eagles from the Spec?" Dilly's eyes were wide.

"Hardly likely. Gold eagles haven't been in circulation for years but the US mint has produced a lot of commemorative coins more recently. Perhaps Captain Finn can tell us more?"

"It's not my area of expertise," Finn said. "The little I know is that they were issued for circulation from the end of the 18th century to the early part of the 1900s. These days they're produced for investment, but the newer coins' value is pretty much the same as gold bullion."

"But what would a coin from the 1800s be worth today?" This time it was Eli asking the question.

"In good condition, easily $5,000 for a $10 coin. There were also half and quarter eagles."

You could almost see Eli's brain working. "Then 10,000 coins today would be worth fifty million dollars! That's staggering."

Chatter about the lost treasures of the world saw us through chocolate mousse with black-sesame ginger ice-cream and fried frangipane with strawberry compote. *Simply heavenly*. Then Dilly announced a fifteen minute break before meeting in the great room to commence the game. Eli and Dodo went outside, whether to smoke or get some air I didn't know. Most of the others hurried to the bathroom; I didn't want to stand in line so I took the opportunity to browse through some of Bert's antiquities. He had a particularly impressive collection of swords and knives featured throughout the great room. There was a beautifully crafted bone-handled knife with a bone sheath called a keris, a curved sword labeled as a katana, British bayonets, hand-crafted daggers, things I'd never heard of or seen before. I made a mental note to ask Bert about them later.

As we began to reassemble, the door from the east patio was flung wide with a terrific gust of wind. Eli and Dodo came in, supporting the maid, Teresa, between them. She looked dazed and shaky. We all stopped what we were doing, hesitant, wondering if this was part of the game, 'til Finn took charge.

"Let's put her on the couch." He took over from Dodo and gently he and Eli laid her down. "What happened?"

"We were heading in," Eli said, "when the kitchen door opened. Teresa must have been coming to check for dirty dishes, I guess, but the wind snatched at the door and just seemed to catch her and spin her around and throw her into the railing."

"I think she hit with her left shoulder," Dodo added.

Finn began to give instructions. "Eli, find Monks and have him bring an ice pack and a glass of water. The rest of you, give the girl some space." He shot a meaningful look at me, which I interpreted as my cue to move everyone away.

"Come on guys. Finn knows what he's doing; he's had medical training so let's leave him to it."

"But what about the game?" Silly Dilly's voice was a little whiney.

"Let's just give it a few minutes." I used my perky voice to try and lighten the mood. "We can always start without Finn and he can catch up later. What do you all say?"

There was a murmuring of assent.

We'd all had to notify Dilly ahead of time who our characters would be. Based on that, dossiers had been prepared describing the characters' backgrounds, objectives and special abilities and were handed around. One of us had been chosen as the victim, though the rest of us didn't know who it would be. When the 'murder' was committed, we could look for clues hidden around the house, and ask each other questions using information in the dossiers.

Neither Finn nor I planned to make any real effort to discover 'whodunit.' After all, we didn't want to win our own prize, so while Dilly was dishing out instructions I let my eyes wander idly around. On the far side of the room, an apparent argument got my attention. The Westgates had Ken Kinimaka cornered. Ralph was taller than Ken by a good six inches. His right arm was over Ken's shoulder with his hand on the wall as Leticia stood to his left. Effectively, they were blocking Ken's movement. There was no way to hear their conversation, and as I was wondering if I should interrupt, they broke apart. At the same time, Dilly gave the 'go' for the game to begin. The excitement was infectious, and I dashed around with the rest of the group looking for the body.

"Over here!" In less than a minute a shout from Dodo brought us all surging to the study where Barbarossa (Bert) lay on the floor with a 'dagger' through his heart. Bert did a sterling job of keeping still while we poked and prodded him for clues, then we broke apart. Everyone went in a myriad of directions in search of solutions to the mystery; I stayed behind briefly to let Bert know he could now get up.

"OK, it's safe."

Bert's eyes opened. "Someone was touching me in places they had no business to be!"

"Hah! I bet I can guess who that was." *Dilly*. "When did you sneak in here anyway? I didn't see you."

"As soon as I saw Teresa wasn't badly hurt and the others were all still distracted, I slipped away. Where is Teresa now? I should go and check on her."

"Not sure, but you might try the kitchen."

So Bert went to find Finn and relieve him, and I took advantage of the fact that no-one was now in the bathroom to relieve myself.

A few minutes later I exited to see Finn coming across the great room towards me.

"How's Teresa?" I asked.

"Bruised and shaken up, but nothing serious. She's back in the kitchen. Now that Bert's corpse gig is over, he said he'd keep an eye on her."

"I know, we talked for a couple of minutes. It's a relief Teresa's not seriously hurt. Let's just hope there are no more accidents."

A loud thump outside caught our attention.

"Sounds like the wind is really picking up out there," I said. The whistling noise it made coming down the chimney reminded me of a nasty little boy at one of the many foster homes I'd stayed in, who used to say it was the banshee coming to take my soul away. I shivered. Time to change the subject.

"Where's the delicious Dilly?"

"I never thought I'd say this, but you have to help get that woman away from me."

"What? A woman you can't handle? Say it ain't so!" I smirked.

"You can laugh. She's all over me like sauce on ribs – and the sauce isn't tasty."

"Apparently the ribs are."

"Phill." Finn's look was becoming desperate. It was tempting to keep teasing him but I decided I'd take pity instead.

"Where is she now?"

"She followed me into the den. When I came out of the kitchen you were all splitting up to look for clues and I was hoping I could just hide out 'til the game was over.

I left her in there. I said I needed to hit the head and escaped."

"Well, fear no more, oh emasculated one, for I have the answer. You may go back into the lion's den with your head held high. Just let Dilly know you're broke."

"That's it?"

I nodded in the affirmative. "Hard to believe, but the woman is not enraptured of the famous Finn charm. She wants you because she thinks you have money."

"If I had, I'd pay her off. But why would she think I'm rich?"

"*Treasure* hunter. Duh!"

Realization began to dawn on his face.

"Right," I continued. "Silly Dilly thinks you get to keep everything you find. She doesn't understand almost all waters are now claimed by some government or another who demand a huge share of any spoils. Or that you have to pay a bunch of lawyers to negotiate with those governments so they don't take everything. Then the backers have to get paid and, after that, there's damn little left to share amongst the divers, who are then liable for tax on their 'earnings.'

"So, go explain. Or even better," I had a flash of inspiration, "ask her for money to back an expedition. That should take care of it."

"Alrighty, then." Finn was looking much happier already.

Suddenly we heard a shriek, and there was the maiden herself, flinging wide the glass doors from the west patio. "There's another one! I found another body!"

Around the great room doors opened and our fellow sleuths reappeared. Like herding animals we followed Dilly outside.

It was Black Bart who lay gutted on the deck, his entrails spilling from his body in a pool of bright red blood.

"That's sooo realistic," I heard Anne Bonny say behind me.

It *was* realistic. Too much so. Then I smelled it; that faint sweet, sickly smell, and there was a slight metallic taste on my tongue.

This wasn't a game anymore. I looked at Black Bart's ruptured body. Shit, he really was dead.

Liz Dodwell

THREE

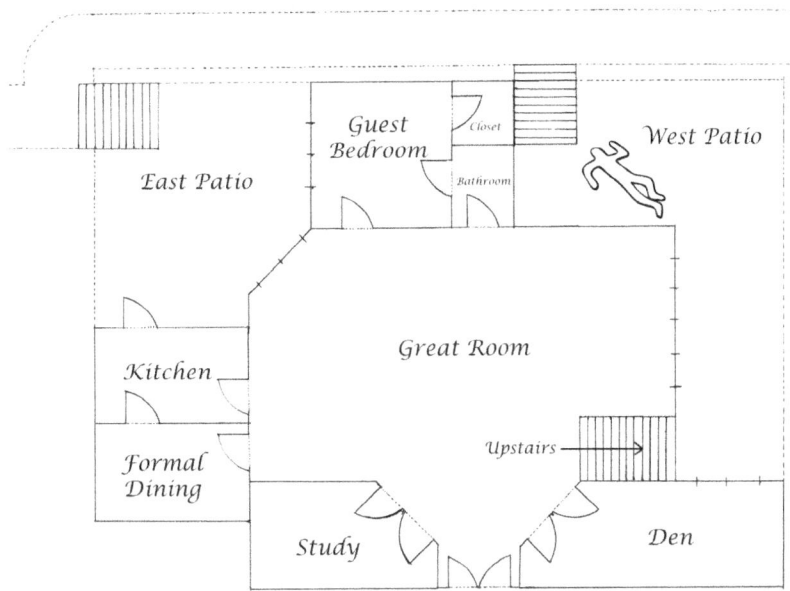

Once again, Finn took charge. "Everybody except Phill and Monks, back into the great room! Now! And nobody leave!"

Hesitantly they began to back away. Whether in shock or mesmerized by the gruesome sight, I couldn't tell. Then Finn yelled 'Now' again and it seemed to jolt everyone awake and they obediently shuffled away.

Finn turned to Monks. "The police need to be notified immediately, but this weather is getting heavy and we're about to get a whole lot of rain. We'll never be able to preserve the crime scene 'til the cops arrive. We may have to move the body. Can you arrange something?"

Monks merely nodded and moved quickly away, though still maintaining a stately air.

"Phill, do you have your cell phone with you?"

"Always." I pulled it from my voluminous skirt.

"Take pictures; as many as you can, from every conceivable angle. Those swells out there," he lifted his chin at the roiling waters, "are only going to get worse. I doubt the police will risk a crossing until the storm passes. Oh, and make sure you get close-ups of that sword. It's no costume piece."

"No, it's not. It's a katana. And it's mine."

Both of us looked round to see Bert standing there. He was obviously pretty shaken but holding it together. "It was hanging on the wall in the great room. I didn't notice it was missing." Then he abruptly changed subjects.

"I have several cameras you could use." He spoke directly to me. "You'll get much better pictures with them."

"I'm strictly a point and shoot photographer. No skills beyond that."

"No problem. I'll help. And Monks will be bringing a tarp so we can move K... er, the body." Bert swallowed hard.

While he and Monks were gone, Finn took a close look at the body. It was on its back with arms flung out to the sides. One leg was bent out at the knee, the other lay straight. The wind was catching at the torn clothing so the wound was completely exposed, with the sword angled in the stomach. I peered over Finn's shoulder and grimaced. "That's a really gruesome cut."

"He's also cut across his fingers on the inside of his left hand."

"Defensive wound maybe?"

"Maybe." If Finn had any thoughts, he was keeping them to himself.

At that moment Bert returned with a camera. He handed it over to me. "Let's do this."

I looked at his white face. "It doesn't need both of us to take pictures. Why don't you join Finn and look around to see if you spot anything out of place."

He looked instantly relieved, as I stepped gingerly around the body, avoiding the blood pool, and began snapping.

As soon as Monks reappeared, Finn gave terse directions. "Lay the tarp out. Bert, you and I will hold it down while Monks and Phill lift the body onto it then we'll each take a corner and carry it like a stretcher. Monks, where are we going?"

"To the den, sir. I've locked the patio doors to the great room from the deck, and left young Mr. Shain guarding the door from the great room to the den. I must tell you, sir, the natives are getting restless. Mr. Westlake is being particularly vocal about his civil rights."

I rolled my eyes. Finn gave a quick shake of his head then commanded us to lift the corpse-laden tarp on a count of three. With reasonable precision we frog-marched along the patio to the den while the raindrops fattened and began to fall faster. We made it through the doors just before Mother Nature hissed her fury down upon us, and lay the body gently on the floor. Bert slid the doors shut and we stood, mutely, gazing at the gored remains, which less than an hour before had been an animated and engaging man.

Of course, Finn was the first to break the mood. "Monks, did you get through to the police?"

"Indeed, sir. I reported the incident immediately and am awaiting a call back with instructions."

"Then there's nothing more we can do right now except seal off the room and let the others know what's going on."

The patio doors were locked and Monks pulled the heavy drapes across. There was a key in the other door; Finn took it and ushered us into the great room before turning the key in the lock and handing it to me. "Put it somewhere safe." So I stuffed it in my bra. *Just let someone try and take it!*

An instant later the room erupted into a caterwauling of complaints from those present, and demands to know what was going on.

Ralph Westgate took the lead. "What's the meaning of keeping us all in here? Where are the police? We're being treated like criminals and I insist you tell us what's happened."

Murmurs of agreement came from the others, their faces a mix of anger and concern.

Finn held up his hands to silence everyone and waited out their mutterings before he spoke.

"As you must know by now, Black Bart is dead. Or I should say, Ken Kinimaka. I ask you to be calm. This has been a shock to all of us, but please keep in mind that Dodo Kinimaka has had the most awful news of all and have consideration for her."

Dodo was curled in an armchair and exhibited no sign of having recognized her name. In her baggy pirate costume she looked like a small turtle that hadn't grown into its shell. The pallor of shock was painted over her face and owlish eyes were dull and unfocused. Wayne Gregory crouched beside her, his tender expression belying a casual acquaintance. Or was I just imagining things?

"Where are the police?" Ralph again, and becoming more belligerent. Leticia clutched at his arm and tried to shush him but he shook her off and glowered at Finn. His loose-limbed frame was now taut and his hands had curled into fists at the end of long ape-like arms. Beside me I sensed Bert and Monks tense in anticipation of trouble with the booze-sozzled Calico Jack, but I had more faith in Finn, who didn't miss a beat.

"Ralph, the police have been notified but I suspect they will be unable to get here until the storm wears itself out, so we need to rely on someone steady and sensible like you to help keep order 'til they make it." *That's it. Appeal to his vanity.*

Ralph's ire immediately deflated and he took on the mantle of authority as one destined for it. Leticia threw a grateful glance at Finn who acknowledged it with the faintest lift at the corner of his mouth.

"Are you saying we have no current contact with the police? Because some of us have been trying our cell phones and we can't get a signal." Heads nodded as Eli asked his question.

"If I may…?" Monks raised his eyebrows at Finn who nodded. "Our private Mud Bug satellite system has a powerful booster and we are able to communicate with the authorities on the mainland."

As if to prove a point, a clapper bell began to ring loudly followed by a guttural voice repeating "Answer ye phone, yer scallywag. Answer ye phone."

Everyone looked a little taken aback and there were a few muted chuckles, while Monks reached into one of the holsters hanging from his costume belt and pulled out a phone.

"Good evening, you've reached Mud Bug Island; Monks speaking……..Yes, detective…………Yes, detective………..He's right here, please hold for a moment."

"Detective Cardero," Monks held the phone out to Finn, "has expressed a desire to speak with you, Captain."

"Hello…..yes, Detective Cardero, this is Rex Finsmer….. Yes, I do remember you……. He's Ken Kinimaka, retired professor….."

"Hey!" Eli shouted out. "Let's all hear what's going on."

A bunch of the others called out in agreement and I couldn't say I blamed them.

Finn waved the voices down. "Detective, I'm going to put you on speaker phone. As you must realize, the other guests are anxious to hear what you have to say." With that he pushed a button and set the phone down on a side table while we crowded round.

"Go ahead, detective."

"This is Detective Lucien Cardero. I'm in charge of this investigation and I want you all to be sure you understand that, because for the next 12 to 24 hours you'll be on your own on the island. Our police launch is unable to navigate the rough waters, so until Tropical Storm Darla passes by and things calm down I'll be conducting the investigation via phone. I am also asking Captain Finsmer to oversee things on my behalf at your end and, assuming he agrees, I expect you to give him your full cooperation."

"What do you mean by 'oversee?'" someone shouted. Eli again, I think.

Then Wayne broke in. "Any chance of getting in by helicopter?"

"There's nowhere to land a copter on Mud Bug," the detective replied, and several people gave Bert dirty looks as if he should have anticipated this. "Meanwhile, I will be conducting telephone interviews with you, which the captain will monitor. He will also...."

"Why Finn? Why not someone else?" Eli just had to keep interrupting.

"Who is that asking?"

"Eli Shain, independent reporter."

"Well, Mr Shain. I've met the captain myself and know his reputation from other police investigations he's helped. I know nothing about you or anyone el......."

There was an enormous crack that resonated through the house and the line went as dead as Black Bart. For a moment everyone stared in shock at the phone lying mute on the table. Then Bert picked it up. "Hello! Hello! Shit. Lightning must have struck the dish."

"Well, so much for that." Eli's lips curled in a sneer.

"I say let Finn do the interviews."

Dilly's suggestion took everyone by surprise, especially coming from her. Almost immediately, Eli denounced the idea; Leticia began to argue in favor and soon voices were raised all around and we were getting nowhere. I'd pretty much had it, so I stood on one of Bert's sturdier antique side tables, raised myself to my full five foot ten and yelled at the top of my voice, "That's enough!"

Ten pairs of eyes turned to me and the voices went quiet.

"Can we please proceed like adults and not a bunch of over-stimulated soccer fans? It's likely one of us is a murderer." Most of the women gasped. Leticia blanched as white as the walls. "We can spend the next 12 hours or so squabbling and looking over our shoulders wondering if we might be next, or let Finn ask a few questions. It certainly can't hurt, and you heard the detective – he trusts Finn, so do I."

"Me, too," Dilly piped up.

"As do I," Bert joined in.

"Let's put it to a vote. All agreed, raise your hands."

With some hesitation nine hands were in the air. Only Eli stood stiffly, arms crossed and lips pursed tightly.

"Come on, Shain." It was Ralph who tried to jostle him into changing his vote. Eli's look was pure stubborn.

"Why would I want an amateur investigating me for murder? For all we know, Finn did it and he could frame any one of us."

"Or you might have done it and you're afraid of the truth coming out." It was said softly and gently but we all heard it. Until now Teresa had stayed in the background but her words caused Eli to color crimson.

"I didn't do it." His demeanor was sullen.

"Then let the captain prove it." She smiled and touched his arm. Eli just caved.

"Alright, then. But only for you."

Well, well. When did that happen? A little romance blooming between the reporter and the maid.

Liz Dodwell

FOUR

Within minutes Finn was set up in the study. He'd insisted he needed me to take notes and no-one had objected. We pooled our own information first and were able to come up with a reasonable time-frame for the killing. I'd seen Ken in the great room just before the game began. That was right around 8.20pm. At 8.35pm, give or take a minute or two, Dilly found Black Bart.

"We need to find out where everyone was during that 15 minutes. The killer had to have the opportunity to remove the katana from the display in the great room *and* do the killing."

"OK, let's get started." I was ready for some real sleuthing.

The first person Finn called was Bert, who walked in looking like a whipped puppy. "Now I know what it's like to be on the wrong side of a lynch mob."

"What's happened?" Finn was sympathetic.

"They act as if it's my fault someone got murdered and ruined their evening. This is why I prefer to be left alone."

Finn's sympathy evaporated. "Snap out of it, man! You're alive and kicking while Ken is dead."

Bert remained glum. "And now I'm going to be grilled as a suspect, I suppose."

"Actually, I'm pretty certain you didn't do it."

Bert perked up as Finn went on. "You were never alone long enough to do the deed. Ken was in the great room just before the game began, and I noticed you slip in here at about the same time. That meant you would have had a minute or two, tops, to run out to the patio, gut him and get back to being a fake corpse. After that, there was always someone with you."

Bert heaved a sigh. "You're right. I'm ashamed I was thinking of myself when someone else suffered a real tragedy. Is there anything I can do to help nail the scum who did this?"

"Actually, there is. Can you print out the pictures Phill took, then help her put them on a board?"

"Easy, but I could set you up a slide show with bigger pictures that would probably be better."

"Finn is still more of a paper and pencil kind of guy." I'd tried to bring him into the light, but he was pretty old-fashioned about some things.

"I know what you're thinking." He gave me a hard stare. "And it's not true. Technology is a wonderful thing but sometimes not the best thing. In this case I want to see all the pictures in a collage in case something pops out at me."

"Yes sir! Anything else, sir?" Bert stood to attention and saluted. *I was really beginning to like this guy.*

Finn didn't react other than to say, "Yes, there is. I want everyone to have writing material so they can make a list of who they remember being in the great room as the mystery game was about to begin, and who they remember being here in the study after the fake corpse – Barbarossa – was found, and where did they go after that. Bert, as the corpse I realize you kept your eyes closed, but do your best to try and figure out who was around based on voices or names you heard.

"Phill, keep an eye on everybody while they do the lists. I don't want them discussing with each other who was where or when. And if Dodo is up to it, ask her to do the same. I'll wait 'til you're done before we call the next witness."

"Or suspect," I mumbled beneath my breath.

Liz Dodwell

FIVE

Ten o'clock and tropical storm Darla was still thrashing around outside. In the study our collage of photographs was set up, as was a slide show of the same pictures on a laptop beside it. With Bert's skills and his advanced computer equipment it took no time to get everything together.

Finn had insisted the others stay together in the great room. "If there is a killer amongst us, that person must not be given the opportunity to manipulate any evidence." Grimly, he'd added, "And there's safety in numbers."

We'd collected the lists Finn had asked everyone to make and were awaiting his instructions.

"Alrighty, then. Here's my list for the great room. I was never in the study with the rest of you. That's when I was taking care of Teresa in the kitchen. I want you both to collate the names so we can see if anybody was missing."

"I get it," said Bert. "One person might remember seven people, another might remember six, but if none of them remember the same character then that could be our killer."

"Exactly," Finn said.

"OK, I can get this done in a few minutes."

Finn frowned. "This isn't something to make light of. It's tedious work and it needs to be done right."

"Nothing difficult at all. I'm going to let the computer do the work."

"By the time you type in all the names you could do the job by hand."

"Type! Who types these days? I'll scan the lists in." With that he was gone.

"I enjoy these moments of techno-revelation with you," I said to Finn.

"We haven't seen the results yet."

Minutes later Bert was back bearing a notebook. "Here's the consolidated report." He propped the machine on the desk. "As you can see, the program sorted through all of the lists and came to the conclusion that everyone was seen in the great room for at least part of the time. As for the study, no-one remembers seeing Ken. Strangely enough, Dilly thinks she saw you Finn, though as we know, you were still in the kitchen with Teresa and Monks, so I think we can chalk that up to wishful thinking on her part." Finn just rolled his eyes.

"Other than that," Bert continued, "I don't know what this tells us."

"It tells us we have a lot of gaps to fill. Let's start bringing everyone in here but, Bert, would you cover the pictures and turn off the slide show. I don't want anyone else seeing that. Then stay with the group and keep your eyes and ears open in case you pick up some useful information.

"Phill, you'll be taking notes."

"Will it help to record the interviews?" Bert asked.

"That's a great idea," Finn responded. "Let's just hope we don't lose power as well as the phone service."

Bert looked pained. "We operate on solar backed up by diesel. If the solar battery banks die, the back-up system will run for another 24 hours. Besides, the notepad has an 11-hour battery life of its own."

"Alright, but Phill, I still want you to take notes and give me your impressions."

Liz Dodwell

SIX

"The others simply don't appreciate what it takes to carry the weight of responsibility. You and I, Finn, are among the few with the character and experience to inspire confidence and bring the best out in others."

Gag me with a spoon, but Ralph Westgate was a pontificating pinhead.

"You know, I'm reminded of a time, about twenty years ago….."

Finn cut him off. "I'd really love to hear about it sometime. Right now, we need to concentrate on Ken's murder."

"Oh, yes. Of course."

"Just for the record, where were you from the time everyone gathered in the great room and until the body was discovered?"

"Well, Leticia and I were together when Eli and Dodo brought Teresa in from the east patio. While you were taking care of her we listened to Dilly's introduction and we were just going over our notes when Barbarossa's body was found, so we followed everyone into the den. After poking around a bit we decided to check out the east patio. I rather thought there might be some significance in what happened to Teresa."

"And was there?"

"We didn't find anything."

"Then what?"

"We heard Dilly shouting and came running with the rest."

"When you were in the great room, did you look at the sword and knife collection."

"No, why do you ask?"

Finn ignored the question and pressed on. "Did you notice anyone else show interest in the collection?"

"No, and I'm not sure I like the tone you're taking with me." *Poor Ralph. Not so sure of himself now.*

"You were seen with your wife talking with Mr. Kinimaka – actually, it was described as arguing – just before Dodo and Eli brought Teresa in from the east patio. Tell me about that."

"It wasn't an argument. We were just discussing his life as a professor."

"That's rubbish." I jumped in. "Things were clearly heated. I'm the one who saw you."

"And," Finn went on, "at dinner, when Ken mentioned Arizona State University, you and your wife both reacted with some surprise."

Ralph's lips tightened to a thin line through which no words could escape. For a long, tense minute we all sat like stone, until Ralph shoved back his chair and stood. "The conversation with Ken had absolutely nothing to do with his death. I have nothing more to say."

He stomped to the door where Finn's voice caught him. "Silence can be far more damning than the truth."

A guttural 'Hmph' was the only response as Ralph slammed the door behind him. I looked at Finn for direction.

"Get his wife in here before he has a chance to talk to her."

I dashed into the great room to see Ralph with a firm hold on Leticia's arm, pulling her away from the study. In a few swift strides I was next to her. "Leticia," I kept my voice even, "Finn would like to speak with you now."

Immediately, Ralph was in my face. "She has nothing to say."

"Look," I began, but Leticia reached up and gently lay the palm of her hand on her husband's cheek.

"Enough, sweetheart. It's time to stop hiding the truth."

Ralph colored and opened his mouth to object but Leticia's expression, though soft, showed resolve. Ralph released his hold and his shoulders slumped as Leticia turned to me. "Shall we go?"

Finn had been standing in the doorway, watching. As we approached he stepped aside and gestured Leticia to a chair. I closed the door behind me and readied myself to take notes.

"My husband is a proud man, Captain. I apologize for his surly behavior but it was motivated by a desire to protect his family, and had nothing to do with Ken Kinimaka's death."

"I need more than that, Leticia. It looked as though you and Ralph were arguing with Ken."

"We weren't arguing with him. We were thanking him."

Finn raised questioning eyebrows; Leticia gave a slight sigh and continued. "Our son, Brian, attended Arizona U and played football there. He was good; good enough that he had a strong chance of being picked up by one of the major leagues. Ralph was thrilled. He was already bragging to everyone about it. But Brian was putting so much into the sport that his grades were beginning to suffer badly. His health was taking a toll, as well: too many sleepless nights trying to study and then pushing himself hard on the field. He did a foolish thing; he paid someone to take his exams for him. Ken Kinimaka found out but, rather than immediately reporting my son, confronted him privately. He told Brian that if he would drop football and concentrate on his studies, he would forget what had happened. Brian accepted Ken's offer and went on to graduate with a 3.8 GPA."

"Then why the heated discussion with Ken?"

"My son never told us who had caught him out. When Ken mentioned Arizona U we saw it as an opportunity to ask him if he knew anything about it. At first he denied any knowledge, but we pressured him and he admitted he was the one."

"I'm still not getting it. Ken apparently destroyed your son's chances of making it to the big leagues. Some people would say that's a good enough reason to commit murder."

Leticia leaned forward and spoke earnestly. "Finn, Ken Kinimaka stopped my son from taking a path to potential destruction. To say I was grateful to him doesn't begin to cut it."

"And does Ralph share your feelings?"

"When Brian first told us about this, Ralph was furious that his son would even consider cheating, and mortified that our friends would find out. But now Brian is a successful businessman with a lovely wife and a baby on the way and he and his father have a great relationship. But Ralph still feels some shame that his son ever considered cheating and it's hard for him to talk about it. I promise you, though, that *both* of us felt nothing but gratitude toward Ken and we're horrified and saddened over what's happened."

"Alright, Leticia." Finn stood and Leticia rose with him. "Thank you for your honesty."

Leticia moved away.

"One more thing," Finn said, and she turned to him. "Did you notice Ken again after you spoke in the great room?"

"That was the last we saw of him."

Liz Dodwell

SEVEN

In quick succession we next had Teresa and Eli in for questioning. Neither had seen anyone near the sword collection or noticed Ken in the great room or study. Teresa had nothing to add except to say she had stayed in the kitchen with Bert until they heard Dilly's shout.

When it was time for Eli to be interviewed, he came into the study huffing and puffing like the big bad wolf. "It's about time. I have important information that could crack this case and you've had me sitting out there with the murderers."

His tone neutral, Finn responded, "Your hot air doesn't blow with me, Mr. Shain. Sit down, please."

Eli glared but sat and proceeded to tell us that he'd overheard a conversation between Dodo Kinimaka and Wayne Gregory in the guest bedroom. "They were talking about a time in Hawaii. Wayne said something about Dodo choosing Ken; Dodo got upset and ran out. A moment later, Wayne ran after her."

"Did you see where they went?"

"They must have gone on to the patio because the doors were open when I came out but I didn't see anyone there."

"And just where did you come out from, Eli?"

"I was in the closet."

"The closet?" I chimed in.

"I was looking for clues."

"Oh, come on. Lurking in a closet seems pretty suspicious to me."

"Like the clues are going to be somewhere obvious? Duh!" *He had a point there.*

"So, Wayne or Dodo next?" I asked Finn as soon as Eli left.

Resting his chin on cupped hands he closed his eyes and was silent in thought for a while. "Let's bring them in together. It might not be a bad idea to see how they react to each other."

They were already together when I went for them; Dodo now so shrunken she seemed in danger of being swallowed by the chair she was in. In contrast, Wayne's posture was tense and inflated, like a wild animal warning predators away.

"Dodo." I squatted before her, gently taking her hand. "Dodo!" I repeated her name with more urgency, but like smoke from a chimney her senses had dissipated and she showed no reaction to her name.

"Let her be," Wayne said. "She's in shock."

Wayne Gregory, I thought, looked like a man whose emotions had been buried alive and could erupt at any moment. It was easy to believe that he had loved this woman for all these years, quietly and perhaps in a suffering sort of way. And now she needed him. Had he made that happen? Was he the killer? I chose my words carefully.

"I promise you Finn will be nothing but considerate. He's the kindest man I know and he's helped many people in times of bereavement. You can come, too. Let's try and put this awful business to rest so Dodo will be able to heal."

Slowly he nodded and spoke Dodo's name, stroking the hair from her face. In an instant, some embers of comprehension returned to her and she gave Wayne a token of a smile.

"Sweetheart, we're going into the study to talk to Finn. OK?"

Mechanically she began to move and we made our way past the other guests who sat still and silent, their eyes following us through the doorway.

An hour had passed. With gentle yet persistent probing and cajoling Dodo had roused herself to answer Finn's questions. And once she and Wayne knew that their conversation in the bedroom had been overheard, their story had been told.

As a Private First Class in the Marine Corps, Wayne had been stationed in Hawaii. There he met the young Dodo and fell in love, but she was already engaged to Ken Kinimaka.

"My parents had pushed for the match. Ken's family had wealth and status and embraced their Japanese roots."

"Just a minute," I said. "Kinimaka isn't a Japanese name."

Dodo continued. "Ken's mother was Japanese but his father had a Japanese mother and Hawaiian father. My situation was similar, and as an obedient Japanese daughter, even though I cared very much for Wayne, I would never have disregarded my parents' wishes."

"Was it a happy marriage?" Finn asked.

"At first it seemed so. Please understand, this was never a love match but Ken was kind to me and I thought when children came along I would have someone to love and who would love me, and everything would be fine. But there were no children. Ken never accused; I just knew he believed it was my fault and for a long time I believed it, too."

"How long?" I asked.

"Six or seven years." Talk about unemancipated.

"Finally, I decided to get tested and, guess what? There was nothing wrong with me. When I told Ken he simply refused to accept it and from then on things got steadily worse. We shared a house though not a home, and not a bed."

At this Dodo glanced briefly at Wayne and a little flush of color rose to her cheeks.

"I'm so sorry, Dodo." Finn cleared his throat. "I understand what a terrible shock this has been to you...."

"No, you don't understand. You don't understand at all. The reason I'm so upset is because a part of me is glad. When I first realized it was Ken who was dead the first thing I felt was relief. For years my life was not good but it wasn't really bad either. I could lose myself in writing and art. I knew Ken had other women – paid prostitutes - and that was fine because it meant he left me alone. All I had to do was play the part of dutiful wife in front of his colleagues. Then this past year I became afraid. He would have wild mood swings, forget whole parts of the day then be angry at me because of it. I wondered if he might have Parkinson's disease because his hands would shake. If I so much as hinted he visit a doctor he'd become enraged. He became obsessed with his ancestry and the supreme role of the male in Japanese society. I...I started to barricade myself into my room...."

Her voice trailed into nothingness.

"Dodo," Finn's voice was low, "you realize this gives you motive?"

Wayne surged to his feet. "That's enough! There's no way she could have wielded that sword. I saw the cut. His belly was sliced open; that took strength."

"The kind of strength *you* have, Wayne?"

Wayne's jaw dropped. At the same moment Dodo's eyes rolled back in her head and she passed out cold.

Liz Dodwell

EIGHT

"So what do you think?" Finn asked.

"I think I need a drink…… and something to eat."

Finn gave me his 'Why am I not surprised' look.

"Hey! All this drama gives a girl an appetite."

Finn had spent another 15 minutes questioning Dodo and Wayne. They claimed that neither of them knew the other would be at the dinner. Dodo said Ken wanted to attend for the chance to rub elbows with some of the local 'elite.' Wayne came because he was a strong supporter of the charity.

Wayne had followed Dodo into the guest room to talk to her when everyone split up to look for clues. She'd become very emotional and run out to the patio and on into the garden. Wayne went after her but lost her. Both denied seeing anyone else until they returned to the house separately.

"So far, that means that neither Dodo nor Wayne, nor the Westgates, have an alibi."

"Include Eli Shain in that list," Finn added.

"So what do you think?"

"I think we need a floor plan of the house. How about you find Bert and see if he's got something."

"Good idea. And I'll see if he's got something to eat."

I was bombarded with questions and complaints as soon as I left the study. Not surprising really. It was closing in on one in the morning. The incessant whine from the wind Darla threw down the chimney as she relentlessly raged outside would drive anyone crazy without the threat of a murderer being in their midst. No-one had managed to sleep and I figured perhaps we all could do with a break before everyone lived up to their pirate alter egos and we had a mutiny on our hands.

After I sent Bert on his mission I grabbed Teresa – I knew I was safe with her – and we headed into the kitchen where we found cold cuts, cheese and other fixings and set about making sandwiches. Rain was hitting the windows with a sharp slapping sound and we had to raise our voices to be heard.

"I'm not surprised you got pulled off your feet." I nodded in the direction of the door to the patio. "Didn't you realize how windy it was?"

Teresa suddenly looked stricken. *What the hell?*

I frowned and fixed my gaze on her. "OK. What gives?"

She bowed her head and mumbled something I couldn't understand. "What?"

"I was supposed to meet Eli there."

"Are you saying you already knew Eli?"

She nodded; then her words came tumbling out. "Eli is my boyfriend. He's here because of me - I work for the catering company that prepared the dinner. When I told him about it he figured if he came he could find out something about Bert or the Westgates or…or even Finn,"

60

here she had the good grace to look ashamed, "and write an expose and make a name for himself."

"Yeah, well I've certainly got a name for him. No wonder he was hiding in the closet; he really was eavesdropping. Why didn't you tell this to us earlier?"

"He didn't mean any harm. He wouldn't hurt anyone. He had to max out his credit card to pay for this. I don't know what he'll do if he can't get a story out of it."

"I don't care. He doesn't deserve a story. And I'm disappointed in you, too. Obviously you were a willing accomplice."

"No," she began to sniffle. "I really didn't want to do this but he said if I loved him I would help."

"Oh, for Pete's sake. Get a grip….. and get a new boyfriend." That said, I snatched a plateful of food and some sodas to take to the study and shoved Teresa ahead of me with the rest of the sandwiches for the hungry pirates.

Bert was with Finn as I re-entered the study, hunched over a blueprint spread on the desk. They looked like they were playing Clue. They had little cutout figures they were moving from room to room.

"I'll take Miss Marple in the dining room with a knitting needle," I said.

Bert looked pained. He held up one of the cutouts. "We're plotting where everyone was at the time of the killing. Each figure represents one of the players."

"And how's that going for you."

"So far, it's not telling us anything new."

"Well, I have something new to tell you." I proceeded to recount my conversation with Teresa. "She seemed genuinely contrite, but it was really stupid of her to get involved."

"It certainly was." Finn grabbed one of the sandwiches and a ginger ale. "It also suggests a motive for Eli."

"You mean he could have killed Ken just so he would have a sensational story to write about?" Bert's face expressed skepticism. "That's pretty far-fetched."

"Agreed. But at this juncture I'm not ruling anything out." Finn pinched the bridge of his nose. He's a five-time cancer survivor and this kind of stress can be really tough on him, but I knew he wouldn't rest until he felt he'd made a breakthrough. He bit into his sandwich and chewed a few times. "What is this stuff?"

"It's called potted shrimp. We found a jar of it in the fridge."

Bert explained. "Monks makes it with small brown shrimp he gets from England, cooked in clarified butter and seasonings. He says it's a British classic."

"It's actually quite tasty."

"I hope *our* Shrimp is OK," I said, at which Bert looked puzzled.

"Shrimp is our cat. She's back at Stock Island on *Time Voyager*. She's probably upset with us being gone during this storm."

Finn snorted. "*Time Voyager* is completely secure, and Shrimp has plenty of food and her choice of beds to sleep in, which is more than we have."

"I guess you're right," I said, and chewed on another sandwich thinking how nice it would be to cozy up next to her warm, fluffy little body and be lulled to sleep by her throaty purr.

Liz Dodwell

NINE

"I assure you, sir, I was not the one who spilled the wine."

"But you apologized for doing so."

"Of course, sir. As butler, one of my primary concerns is to ensure the comfort and pleasure of guests. If that means I take responsibility for an accident caused by a guest then so be it. However, in light of Mr. Kinimaka's unfortunate demise, I feel it incumbent upon me to inform you it was Mr. Kinimaka who spilled the wine. I had noticed earlier that he had an occasional involuntary tremble in his right arm. He had reached for his glass just after it was filled. His hand jerked and sent the glass rocking: enough to spill some of its contents, though without falling over."

Idly, I wondered if it was a requirement at butler school to speak 'posh.'

"Tell me about the coin, Monks."

"There is little to tell. It's a family token that was given to me by my father, who had it from his father and so on."

Finn held out his hand. "May I see it?"

With some reluctance Monks removed the chain from around his neck and placed it in Finn's hand.

"The date is 1842, which means it could be part of the horde from the Spec."

"I don't know its origin, sir."

"You know more than you're telling us. It was clear when Ken mentioned his family finding the cache of Gold Eagles that it resonated with you. Speak out, man."

"Go ahead, Monks," Bert urged. "No-one here is going to jump to conclusions."

"Alright, sir. Here's the story that's been told in my family.

"About five generations back my ancestor was a sailor on board the Spec. With two other men he was charged with guarding a chest of coins – payment for a delivery of opium – while the rest of the crew and the captain were ashore, living it up. One of the men forced my ancestor at gun point to help him steal the treasure after he'd drugged the third sailor. The man had an accomplice who rowed out to the schooner with a bunch of ballast rocks that they exchanged for the coins.

"They gave my ancestor the choice to stay on board or come with them to the island. He knew, of course, if he stayed he'd be lynched when it was found the coins were missing, so he took his chances with the thieves. Once they reached land, the thieves tossed him a single coin and told him to keep his mouth shut or they would find him and kill him. He took the coin and ran. When morning came, in spite of warning skies, the Spec's captain decided to sail. Perhaps his judgment was impaired by the previous evening's alcoholic intake; at any rate, as Ken told you, the ship was caught in the storm and went down in 700 fathoms. My ancestor came forward and said he'd been on board and managed to swim to safety. Strangely enough, the other crewman, the thief, did the same. They were believed to be the only two 'survivors.'

"Both men later gained passage on another schooner from Honolulu to the Malay Peninsula. My ancestor just wanted to get away; the thief presumably was laying a cover story and planning to return and claim his booty. What happened after that I have no idea, except my family used the coin as a talisman to remind us that hard work and honesty is always best."

Finn sat back, stroking his beard; a habit he had when deep in thought. It seemed a hell of a coincidence that two men whose ancestors had been involved in a crime more than 160 years ago should now find themselves in the same place at the same time, and one of them would be killed.

"Fifty million dollars is a hell of a motive for revenge," Finn said.

"My ancestor was *not* a thief. And, in fact, his coercion into the deed was a stroke of luck - he would otherwise have been on board when the Spec sank. My feelings toward Mr. Kinimaka would naturally be gratitude rather than revenge."

"Alright, Monks. That will do for now."

The man gave a curt nod, turned smartly and exited.

"Well," I said, "it looks to me as if he had motive but did he have opportunity? He was seen in the great room and the den but we can't pinpoint a time. Maybe he took the sword down before we got here. I looked at the collection but I couldn't tell you if the katana was there or not."

"I have to say something." Bert was agitated. He took a deep breath then let it out slowly before continuing. "Apart from the fact that I know Monks and I know he didn't do this, there would be no reason for him to use a sword to kill anyone. He's ex-SBS. That's Special Boat Service, the British Naval Special Forces. They're among the best of the best. Monks could kill someone fifty different ways with just his bare hands."

"How does an ex Special Forces man come to be working for a reclusive multi-millionaire?" Finn asked, while I was trying to come up with just ten ways to kill a person bare-handed.

"Believe it or not, people with Monks' skill set can have a tough time finding work when they leave the military. He went to the Butler's Academy, which is where I found him when he graduated. Making a lot of money also makes you a target for a lot of freaks and Monks, with his abilities, was just what I needed."

"And yet he let a murder happen," I murmured.

"Yes." Bert hung his head. "He's pretty angry with himself about that – and with me. He was against this event from the beginning. Said it would be impossible to perform his butling duties and at the same time keep an eye on ten strangers who had the run of the house. So he concentrated on my safety and Ken got killed. Monks really can't be blamed for that."

"I just had a thought." *Why hadn't this occurred to me before?* "Could Bert be the real target? After all, he's the one with the big bucks. Maybe Ken saw something and the killer had to shut him up."

Finn stroked his beard: he does that when he's deep in thought. Then he uncovered the pictures and looked intently at them. Bert was about to speak but I shook my head at him. When Finn is like this it's best to leave him alone, so Bert and I shoved figures around on the blueprint hoping something new might jump out at us. It didn't.

Liz Dodwell

TEN

"I'm missing something." Finn practically growled. "There's something there but I can't quite see it."

He turned from the photos. "Who do we still have to talk to?"

"Only Dilly."

He rolled his eyes. "OK. Before we bring her in, let's have a quick recap. I don't think Bert was the intended victim. Everything about this smacks of a crime of opportunity. Why would someone plan to kill a person when they're on a small island with a dozen people around? Better to wait for Bert to come to the mainland, use a high-powered rifle from a distance or run him down with a fast bike. There are lots of better ways to do it."

"Thanks," Bert said.

Ignoring him, Finn went on. "So let's continue on the premise that Ken was the killer's target. Who had motive. Phill?"

I took my cue. "First off, there's Dodo. Her marriage was a sham and Ken had become threatening of late. Maybe she stands to get a nice insurance policy on his death."

"Who else?"

"Wayne, of course. He suddenly finds the love of his life again, sees how unhappy she is and decides to take matters into his own hands.

"Then there's Monks. Sorry, Bert." I gave him an apologetic look. "We only have his word that his family never wanted the treasure."

"But we don't know that the thief was actually Ken's ancestor. Ken said his family *found* the coins. It's quite possible the thief never came back to Hawaii to claim his fortune," Bert was pleading hard for his protector, "so why would Monks want to harm an innocent person?"

"Point taken, Bert," Finn said. "For now we're just making a list of possibilities, and we need to put Eli on it as well. People have been murdered for a lot less than an opportunity to make a name for themselves."

"Doesn't that mean Teresa also had motive?" I asked. "She pretty much admitted she'd do anything for Eli. And what about the Westgates? They *said* they were grateful to Ken for forcing their son out of the football program. Maybe they really resented his interference. Ralph Westgate obviously isn't a man who readily admits mistakes."

"Killing for pride? I suppose anything's possible. Where does all this leave us?" Finn looked at Bert.

"We have Dodo, Wayne, Monks, Eli, Teresa, Ralph and Leticia."

"Cross Teresa off. She was with someone the whole time, so it couldn't be her."

"Would Dodo be strong enough to do the deed?" I wondered.

"A woman in a rage can draw on amazing strength."

I looked at Bert in surprise. *How would he know that?*

"Let's keep moving forward," said Finn. "Who had opportunity?"

The three of us studied the blueprint. There was a brief period of time before I came out of the bathroom and met Finn coming from the den when the great room had apparently been empty, and anyone could have gone unseen to the west patio. Moreover, with the exception of Monks, any of our suspects could have slipped along the garden path from the west to the east patio.

"Here's what's still confusing me," I said. "How did the murderer know Ken was on the west patio? I mean, everyone except Ken seems to be accounted for at the time the fake Barbarossa body was found. So did the killer see Ken go out before that? And why was Ken there anyway, before we'd started the game? And why pick that sword? Wouldn't a dagger be easier to use – and to hide?"

"There's about to be another murder." Bert was shaking his head in frustration at me.

"What did I do?"

"Just complicated things even more with all your questions."

"Maybe not." Finn was looking like someone for whom the sun was just about to shine.

"I know that look. What? What is it? You figured out something."

"Just a thought."

"Well tell us!"

But he just shook his head - *I hate when he does that* – and suggested it was time to get Dilly.

"Fine. Let's do Dilly."

ELEVEN

It had just occurred to me why Dilly thought men liked her. When she talked, they were silent. No doubt she imagined they were listening; in fact, I'm sure they were tuning out. The woman kept up an incessant monologue of utter drivel. I'd had better conversations with a talking parrot.

She sat in front of the desk, legs crossed neatly, looking as well-put-together now as the beginning of the evening, which was hours ago. It had just passed four in the morning.

Finn stood and walked around the desk, hiking his backside on the edge and looking down at Dilly. She stopped talking and returned his gaze.

"Dilly, I need you to focus and answer a few questions."

"Of course," she flashed a smile she'd probably spent hours practicing in the mirror. Finn pressed on.

"We know you were present in the great room and then the study when Barbarossa was found. After that, you and I were briefly together in the den. Would you tell me what you did and where you went after I left?"

"Well, I waited a few minutes and when you didn't come back I peeked out the door and saw you talking with Phill. You looked pretty serious so I didn't want to disturb you, but that left nowhere else to go but the patio – the west patio. Of course, as game organizer my role is to oversee the players and nudge them towards a clue, if necessary, so I decided to check and see if anyone was out there. That's when I found… um….. you know."

Bert and I exchanged glances. However unintentional, Dilly had just told us she had the opportunity to kill Ken. *What about motive?*

"Dilly, did you know Ken before this evening?"

Her eyes narrowed. "I met him once before," she said vaguely.

"Did something happen then?"

Squirming a little she replied, "Not really. It was just a party at The Villa by Barton G." *Whoa. High Society at the former Versace Mansion in Miami Beach.*

"Dilly, if something happened it's better you tell me now. The police will find out later anyway."

"Oh, alright. I overhead Ken telling some people that my husband obviously didn't marry me for my intellect, because the size of my brain certainly didn't measure up to the size of my breasts."

There's motive. Flimsy, but still motive.

Dilly went on. "I know I'm not the smartest person. I didn't go to college and my family were poor, but I'm still a *good* person. It was cruel of Ken to talk about me like that. I would never say such unkind things about anyone else."

A little tinge of guilt was coming over me. I'd made fun of Dilly behind her back when she'd been nothing but kind to me. And truth to tell, I couldn't see her wielding a sword to slice and dice someone and risk breaking a nail. *Ouch. There I go again.*

"Can I go now?" Dilly asked.

Finn nodded and she rose. At the door she turned. "You know, just once it would be nice if someone considered my feelings. Even though I didn't care much for Ken, it was a terrible shock to find him like that. I was really sick to my stomach and I can't shake the image of him lying there, gutted and bloody. It was so gruesome and so.... oh, I don't know..... so ritualistic." And with that she left.

As I turned back to Finn he clapped his hand to his forehead and his eyes went wide. "I've been such an idiot." He flung back the sheet that covered the pictures and peered closely at them. Neither Bert nor I dared utter a word before Finn spoke.

"Have either of you been wondering why no-one had any blood on them?"

We shook our heads. I felt like an idiot for not considering that, and I suspect Bert felt much the same.

"Well, I have. And Dilly just told me why."

Huh?

"I think the time has come to unveil the killer."

Liz Dodwell

TWELVE

Darla had finally had her fill of us and was moving on. The wind was now a hum, not a roar, and though the air was still heavy with wetness the last sprinkling raindrops had ceased. It was an hour before sunrise.

In the great room there was an air of tense expectancy. Coffee had been brewed and we'd all roused ourselves to form a rough semi-circle around Finn. He alone stood, relaxed, his face unreadable. The last of the chatter died down and into the silence Finn spoke.

"A murder mystery dinner and the mock killing of the pirate Barbarossa; a game that began in light-hearted fun. Then the game turned deadly, with the real killing of Calico Jack – Ken Kinimaka, a retired history professor. Who would want to kill such a man?

"As it happened, there were motives galore to choose from. A wife in a loveless marriage," he looked at Dodo then Wayne, "or did her ex-lover slay the husband to release her from her torment?

"We have the young reporter and his girlfriend." Teresa averted her eyes while Eli glared defiantly. "To what lengths might they go to create a sensational story they could later sell?

"Then we have Ralph and Leticia Westgate, whose son was caught by Ken cheating on a college exam. They say they were grateful to Ken, but perhaps that's a lie. Perhaps the embarrassment of their son being exposed as a cheat still stings. Enough that they would conspire to kill a man? Maybe."

"How dare you." Ralph was on his feet. Leticia clutched at his arm. "Please, Ralph."

"Sit down, Mr. Westgate!" Finn didn't raise his voice but his tone spoke of such authority that Ralph slowly sank into his chair. When everyone's attention was back on him, he picked up his narrative.

"Next was Dilly. She had been shamefully humiliated by Ken. Is she the sort of person to kill in retribution for such behavior?

"Lastly, there is Monks. With a tale of treasure, lost then found, could this be an act of vengeance?"

Finn shook his head. "So many motives, yet would any of them be sufficient to commit murder? And all of these people, with the exception of Teresa, appear to have had the opportunity to do so. There were a few brief minutes after Barbarossa's body was found and the game began in earnest that the great room was empty. Someone could quickly have slipped unseen to the west patio and struck Ken down. Then again, Dodo, Wayne, Eli or the Westgates could have dashed along the garden path from the east to the west patio."

"We did no such thing!" Ralph, again.

"Then tell me this. Why did you not mention seeing Dodo and Wayne come from the guest room while you were outside? They've both admitted they crossed the patio down to the garden. You must have seen them if you were there."

Ralph looked ready to explode but it was Leticia who responded. "We didn't see anyone because we also went into the garden. Ralph was rather drunk," she gave him the look wives reserve for their husbands when enough is enough, "so I made him walk around to sober up a bit."

"Again, so many people with apparent motive and opportunity. Too many it seemed. And too many unanswered questions. Who took the katana from Bert's collection, and when was it taken? How did the killer know Ken was on the west patio? And where was the blood? I don't mean blood on the body; I'm referring to blood on the killer. There was certainly some spatter. How did the killer avoid it? At last, something Dilly said made me realize I'd asked the wrong question."

"Me?" Dilly was more surprised than the rest of us.

"Yes, Dilly. You were smarter than all of us. You noticed something no-one else did. You said the killing looked ritualistic. That's when it struck me the question was not 'who took the katana,' but 'why take the katana.' After that, everything fell into place.

"The katana, as Bert tells me, was used in feudal Japan and is often referred to as the 'Samurai sword.' We learned from Dodo that Ken had become obsessed with his Japanese ancestry; he would have recognized the katana as a traditional Japanese sword. When Ralph and Leticia were talking to Ken they were standing right by the sword collection. It would have been easy for Ken to grab the katana without being noticed when the game began and we were all concentrating on finding clues. And if he *was* seen with the sword he could have joked that he wanted to be like a real pirate with a real sword."

"I don't understand," Leticia said. "Why would Ken take the sword?"

"You remember my other question? How did the killer know where Ken was? Because Ken *was* the killer."

There were collective gasps and cries of 'How?' 'What?' 'Suicide?'

Finn held up his hands to silence everyone. "Yes, suicide. But a ritual suicide. That's what Dilly saw when none of us did."

Again, there were calls of how and why.

"Here's what I believe happened. It's unlikely Ken came here planning to kill himself, but it might well have been on his mind for some time. When he noticed the katana he took the opportunity to end his life in a way he felt befitted his heritage – hara-kiri."

"How could you make that assumption?" Wayne threw his hands out in a gesture of skepticism.

"I assure you, I assumed nothing. In hara-kiri, or seppuku, which is self-disembowelment, the abdomen is slit open from the left to the right. The blade is then turned upward. That's how we found Ken, with stomach slit horizontally and the sword blade facing upward."

"For God's sake, man, Dodo doesn't need to hear this." Wayne's protective instincts were on full throttle.

"It's OK, Wayne. I want to know what happened. I'm part Japanese, too, remember. I understand the traditions; even those that are as distasteful as this." She nodded at Finn to keep going.

"Another reason I'm convinced Ken did this is because of the cuts on his left hand. Traditionally, a short sword would be used but the katana is a mid-length weapon, which makes it more difficult to use. I think Ken held the hilt in his right hand and wrapped his left around the actual blade so he could make a stronger, steadier cut."

"But why?" Eli asked the questions on all our minds. "Why would he kill himself at all? And why now, and why in such a bizarre way? He was a well-respected and successful man."

"An autopsy will have to be conducted and, when it is, I strongly suspect it will be found that Ken was in the late stage of neurosyphilis. Syphilis can be in the body for years without exhibiting any obvious symptoms. When it affects the brain it can cause altered behavior and impaired movement that can easily be mistaken for Parkinsons's disease. Ken had a problem at times with shakiness and had recently begun to experience extreme, even dangerous, mood swings.

"For years, he had been intimate with prostitutes, which is where he probably contracted the disease. I'm sure he must have known what was wrong with him but his pride had never allowed him to seek medical help. Add to that he had been unable to father a child, yet had always publicly blamed Dodo; I believe he had begun to feel deep remorse for his actions and his unkind treatment of his wife.

"As for why now?" Finn shrugged. "A simple case of opportunity. Dodo has told us that Ken was obsessed with his Japanese ancestry. He must have seen the katana and recognized it as a samurai sword. I can only surmise it triggered in his damaged mind the idea to gain atonement for his errors. Hara-kiri requires enormous physical courage. For a samurai warrior it was a way of regaining some measure of honor."

No-one spoke and no-one moved. After hours without sleep, and the fear and stress of being in the company of a murderer, they were pretty much shell-shocked.

The first to move was Monks who went over to the patio doors and pulled back the curtains and opened the doors. Early rays of pale sunlight filtered in with a welcome taste of morning air. In the quiet we heard the cough of a motor and muted voices.

"I believe the police have arrived," the butler said. "Perhaps I should greet them."

"Yes, do," Finn said. *Do indeed.*

THIRTEEN

"Well, that's it. We'll be ready to go at first light." Finn stretched before settling himself on the settee in *Time Voyager*'s salon. One really good thing had come out of the bloody affair a few nights ago – at least, for me and Finn – Bert had offered us a berth at Mud Bug Island for as long as we liked and at no cost. The little marina he'd built was equipped with electricity and potable water – it was perfect. With the money we'd save on docking fees we'd be able to get the mailbox blowers we wanted sooner rather than later.

Oh, for those of you not familiar with treasure-hunting equipment, blowers are tiltable metal tubes on the boat's stern. They force a jet of prop wash to the bottom and can remove centuries of overburden from shipwrecks buried in sand, saving hours and hours of work that would otherwise have to be done by hand.

Anyway, it was our last night at Stock Island. I'd enjoyed staying there. We'd made friends with some really good people, especially the shrimpers. "I can't say I'll miss the *smell* of shrimp, though," I said, at which point Shrimp appeared, thinking I'd called her name. I picked her up and scratched her nose. "Think she'll like Mud Bug?"

"She'll be in kitty heaven."

Abruptly I switched subjects. "I created a new cocktail with a pirate theme. Most people think of pirate loot in terms of gold coins and jewels, but food and other things would have been at least as important. So this has chocolate vodka, blue curacao and orange bitters to represent sugar, cocoa and indigo. I'm calling it Blackbeard's Folly."

"Sounds good to me. I'll try one."

Off I went to mix and shake. When I came back I handed Finn a glass and seated myself beside him. For some time we sat in companionable silence, each with our own thoughts. Mine went back to the arrival of the police on Mud Bug. It had been some hours before they were willing to accept Finn's hypothesis of what happened to Ken Kinimaka. The pictures we'd taken and our notes were, of course, seized; Ken's body was examined before being bagged and removed. Bert was given a receipt for the katana, though he said he wasn't sure he'd want it back.

Eventually, we were all allowed to leave and Finn and I gratefully drove back to *Time Voyager*. Shrimp was pretty miffed at having been left alone for so long, but she soon forgave us. Maybe because I gave her an extra-large portion of her favorite food.

We'd had a call earlier in the day from Detective Cardero. He was passing along an official 'thank you' from the department, he told us. Also, he wanted Finn to know he'd been right about Ken having syphilis, and the coroner had concluded the wound was self-inflicted. "Even though the circumstances are dreadful, it's still nice to know you're right," Finn had said.

By now I'd finished my Blackbeard's Folly and so had Finn.

"What did you think?"

"Pretty good."

"Want another one?"

"Alrighty, then."

The end

Captain Finn Treasure Mysteries is an ongoing series, though each book contains an individual story.

Become part of the in-crowd and get a FREE short story:
http://lizdodwell.com/signup/

Find all of Liz's books here:
http://lizdodwell.com/books/

Liz Dodwell

AUTHOR'S NOTES

I so hope you enjoyed *Black Bart is Dead,* because I really worked hard on this story. It may be short but it took a good bit of planning, moving stick figures around a floor plan to be sure all the suspects could have done the deed. At any rate, dear readers, please consider leaving a review wherever you purchased this book. As an independent author it's not easy to compete out there and I'd really appreciate your feedback. And please join me, I'd love to get to know you at www.facebook.com/LizDodwellAuthor.

For you treasure-hunting buffs, the *Spec* was a real opium runner that sank in the Kaulakahi Channel between Kauai and Niihau in 1846, apparently with a chest of $10 gold eagles. In her earlier life the schooner was named *Independence.* She was 86 foot long, with a beam of 22 feet. In 1838 she was rechristened the *Flying Fish* and became part of the Wilkes Expedition squadron, exploring the South China Seas for four years until she was declared unseaworthy and condemned. Before being dismantled however, she was purchased and put into service for smuggling. She sank, with the gold, in 700 fathoms (that's deep; a fathom is six feet). Two crewmen reportedly survived.

The organization SAV is completely an invention of my mind. However, I do want to mention there are some great groups who actually do rescue shelter animals and train them to help wounded warriors. A couple are *Paws & Stripes*, and *K9s for Warriors*. They do wonderful things. Why not look them up? And if you know of similar groups, please give them a shout-out on my facebook page.

Once again I want to thank Captain Carl Fismer for his inspiration and friendship these many years. If you want to know anything about shipwreck treasure hunting, he's your man. Find him here: http://www.carlfismer.com.

Thanks to everyone who gives me ideas and criticism (of the constructive variety); to my invaluable assistant, Dominic Ottaviano; and as always, my husband, Alex Markovich, who thinks everything I write is wonderful (I'm so lucky).

The end

Become part of the in-crowd and get a FREE short story:
http://lizdodwell.com/signup/

Find all of Liz's books here:
http://lizdodwell.com/books/

The Gold Doubloon Mystery

ONE

The first of the reef sculptures was ready to be lowered into the water. The cremated remains of a woman had been mixed with environmentally-safe concrete and formed into a huge starfish, which now hung over the side of the boat. We hadn't known the woman in life, nor did we know any of her family who had gathered to watch her take her place amongst the sea life. We were there to memorialize the life of Ned "Guppie" Zawacki, an old-time treasure-hunting friend and mentor of Finn's. Ned had died without family, and pretty much broke. In fact, Finn and I were about the only people there for him at the end, and it was Finn who had commissioned the bell-shaped tribute that would become part of the artificial reef. By the way, in case you're wondering about the Guppie moniker, it's because of the way Ned used to purse his lips when he was thinking hard.

Sea Spirit Reef was about three miles off the coast of Jupiter in Florida. It was loosely modeled after Port Royal, Jamaica, which sank into the ocean back in the late 1600s after a massive earthquake. You might think the theme a bit off-key as a memorial, Port Royal having been notorious for pirates, prostitutes and booze and all. But there are nearly 2,000 of these reefs throughout the country, so having just one for those of us who like things a little quirky is OK in my book.

So, back to the story. We were respectfully waiting our turn to send Ned into the sea that he loved, along with about a dozen other small groups. A couple of divers were in the water, ready to guide the concrete starfish to its final destination. The rope around the sculpture had been crackling with the tension of its weight when, suddenly, it snapped. The starfish plunged into the water, narrowly missing one of the divers. A couple of women screamed, while most of us were momentarily immobilized in surprise.

Finn was the first to recover, rushing to the side to make sure the divers were OK. The rest of us streamed after him and peered into the depths. Two distinct sets of bubbles rose where the two divers were no doubt working to set the sculpture in place. "What's that?" someone said, pointing to another slight disturbance on the surface; nothing much, just a circular rippling really. Then something broke through the ripples and settled gently into the rhythm of the sea.

"Is that a fish?" an uncertain voice asked.

We all strained forward a little more to see better. This time, a lot of people screamed as they realized it was no fish. It was a body.

Liz Dodwell

…was told so many times that she really knew how to spin a yarn, she finally decided to put that talent to good use. Taking inspiration from her good friend and real-life treasure hunter, Captain Carl Fismer, she created the Captain Finn Treasure Mystery series.

For several years Liz worked with the Captain, operating his website and arranging talks and treasure exhibitions. "I would dive when I got the chance, but only on a hookah," she says. "I never found anything of real importance, but just knowing I was getting even a microscopic glimpse of history and adventure was truly exciting."

Fueled by an occasional cup of grog, Liz writes from the home she shares with husband Alex and a crew of rescued dogs and cats. For a change of pace she pens stories in cozy mystery and romantic suspense. For relaxation she likes to yodel. (Just kidding).

www.LizDodwell.com

www.ingramcontent.com/pod-product-compliance
Lightning Source LLC
Chambersburg PA
CBHW070529130626
46555CB00003B/1337